Rainbow Fish & Friends

SCAREDY-CAT FISH

TEXT BY GAIL DONOVAN

ILLUSTRATIONS BY DAVID AUSTIN CLAR STUDIO

Night Sky Books
New York · London

W9-BAY-073

"Come on, Puffer," pleaded Rainbow Fish after lunch one day. "Tell us a story."

Puffer puffed himself up. "It was a dark and stormy night," he began. "The kind of night when ghosts swim up from the Deep."

"Don't tell a ghost story!" cried Dyna. "I don't like those." She knew a real scientist shouldn't believe in ghosts, but she couldn't help it.

"Scaredy-cat!" teased Spike. Dyna swished her tail in a huff.

"I wonder what's really down in the Deep?" asked Tug.

Nobody knew the answer. Little fish were not allowed to leave the shallow, sunlit waters of the Coral Reef and swim down into the dark, cold Deep. Rainbow Fish and his friends knew that Jonah the whale patrolled the edge of the reef and kept everyone safe—but none of them had ever seen him.

"I'm not afraid of the Deep," boasted Spike. "I'm not afraid of anything!"

"Everyone's afraid of *something*," said Tug. "Sometimes I worry about getting lost—just like that time in the Crystal Caverns."

"Me, too," said Rusty.

"I'm afraid of sea storms," said Rosie. "I don't like all the thunder and lightning."

"Me, too," said Rusty.

"Well, I don't like acting on stage," Puffer admitted, "but that's because I'm a million times better backstage."

"Me—"

"We know Rusty!" the friends cried in unison.

Spike laughed at all of them. "What a bunch of scaredy-cats."

"I am *not* a scaredy-cat," said Dyna. "I know it's silly to be afraid of ghosts—I know they're not real. That's why I play at the Sunken Ship. I'm trying to face my fear head-on. It's not scientific to be afraid."

"Scaredy-cat, scaredy-cat," sang Spike.

"Quit it, Spike," said Rainbow Fish. He didn't like the way Spike was teasing everyone, and he was nervous that Spike would pick on him next. Rainbow Fish didn't want to say his fear out loud. Luckily, Miss Cuttle rang the bell and it was time to go back to class.

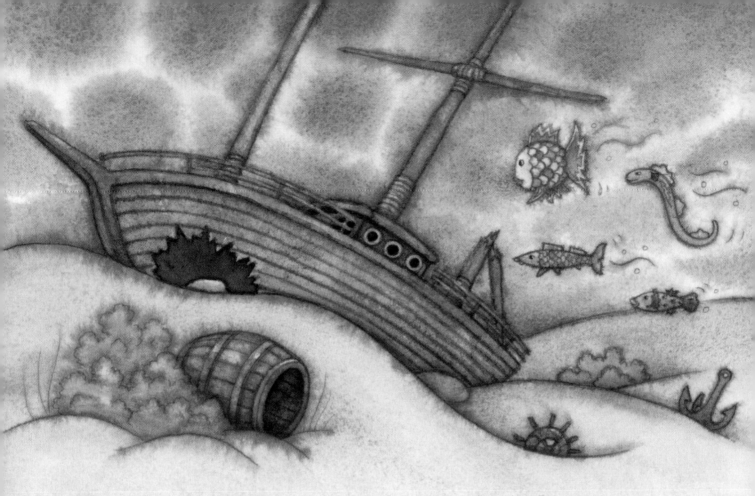

All afternoon, Rainbow Fish thought about what Dyna had said. Maybe his fear was silly, too. Maybe she was right. Maybe he should try and face his fear.

After school Rosie called, "Hey Rainbow Fish, come play follow the leader!"

"Sorry," said Rainbow Fish. "I can't. I have something I have to do."

"Can I come?" asked Tug.

Rainbow Fish smiled. "Not this time, Tug. I have to do this by myself. But thanks."

Rainbow Fish swam and swam and swam, until he reached the edge of the reef. There it was. What he feared most—the Deep. What was down there? he wondered. Would it be friendly to a small fish with a silver scale? Rainbow Fish knew there was no turning back. It's now or never, he thought. Time to face my fear. He swam forward.

Suddenly a gigantic shape rose up from the depths of the water.
Rainbow Fish couldn't move, or speak, or even think what to do. The
shape came closer and closer . . .

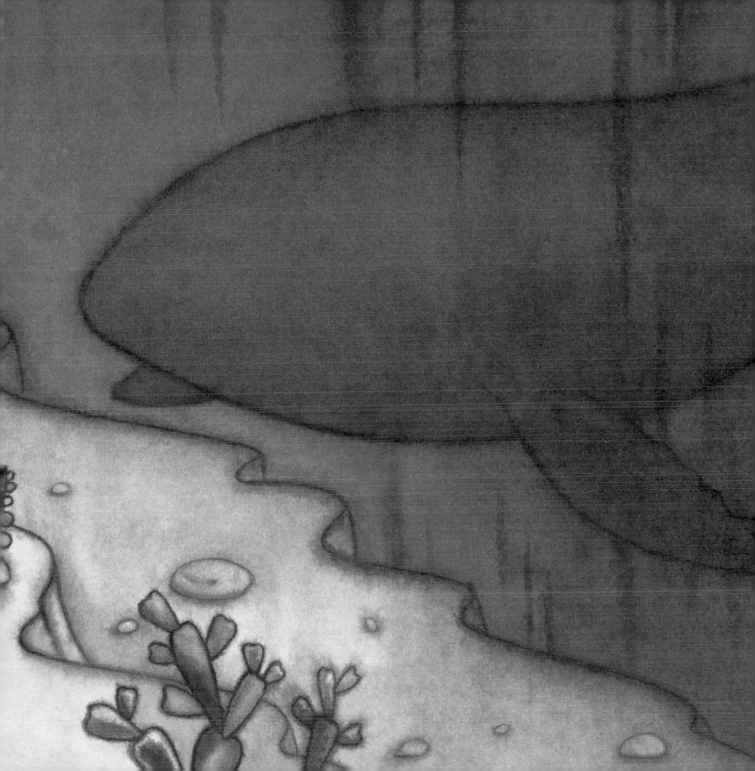

"Hello, Rainbow Fish," a large voice boomed. "What are you doing way out here at the edge of the Deep, where little fish don't belong?" Rainbow Fish looked up and saw that the huge voice belonged to a giant whale.

"Jonah," he whispered, relieved.

Rainbow Fish told Jonah the whole story.

"Not all fears are silly," said Jonah when Rainbow Fish had finished. "If you hear a little voice inside your head telling you something might be dangerous, then listen to it! That little voice is called common sense. Listen to yourself—not to friends who tease you or call you names!"

Rainbow Fish nodded. He felt a lot better.

"I'll watch you swim home now," said Jonah. "Remember, I'm always here watching out for you—but I want you to watch out for yourself, too."

"Weren't you afraid?" asked Rusty the next day, when Rainbow Fish told his friends all about going to the edge of the Deep.

"Yes," said Rainbow Fish. "But Jonah said it shows good common sense to be afraid sometimes."

"Hah! You mean *non*sense," said Spike. "I'm still not afraid of anything."

"Look," said Rosie. "A flying fern."

"A-A-A-H-H-H! Get it off!" roared Spike, as the plant fluttered onto his fins. "Quick! Get it off me!"

"It's just a harmless little plant," said Dyna. "It can't hurt you."

"Yeah, but they're so sticky . . . I mean I—" Spike stammered.

"Is that your 'little voice' talking, Spike?" Rosie asked, giggling.

Spike laughed, too. "Yeah, I guess it's telling me it's okay to be a scaredy-cat."